This book belongs to

Presented by

Patch the Hill Country Bunny
Copyright © 2019 by Mary Delmore Balagia. All rights reserved.
ISBN 978-1-941515-99-0
Library of Congress Control Number: 2018963613

Published by LongTale Publishing
www.LongTalePublishing.com
6824 Long Drive Houston, Texas 77087

LongTale® is a registered trademark of LongTale Publishing.

Photography and photo editing by Mary Delmore Balagia
Photo editing advisor: Sandra Freeman
Background patterns © Kastanka for Adobestock.com
Author photos by Sarah Austin

Design by Monica Thomas for TLC Book Design, www.TLCBookDesign.com
In-house editor: Sharon Wilkerson

Printed in Canada

To Emilia,
stay curious, continue to explore
and always remember…
your Honey loves you.

This is the story of Patch.

One day, Patch received an invitation to visit her
grandmother Honey Bunny in the Hill Country of Texas.

She lived in a big city with bright, flashing lights
and cars that zoomed and boomed as they went by.
Patch thought the country must be just the same,
but she was in for a big surprise!

Patch hopped into her little,
red car and headed to the country.

Her ears flopped as she
drove down the dusty,
brown road.

Along the way, a big, yellow grasshopper sprang into view. Patch stopped her car to let the grasshopper move on.

As Patch waited, she noticed the sights and sounds of busy insects all around her. It was different from the blinking lights and honking horns of the city.

Bees buzzed in the center of bright, orange poppies.

A spider quietly spun a web that gleamed in the golden sunlight.

When Patch arrived at her grandmother's house,
she found a note on the door.

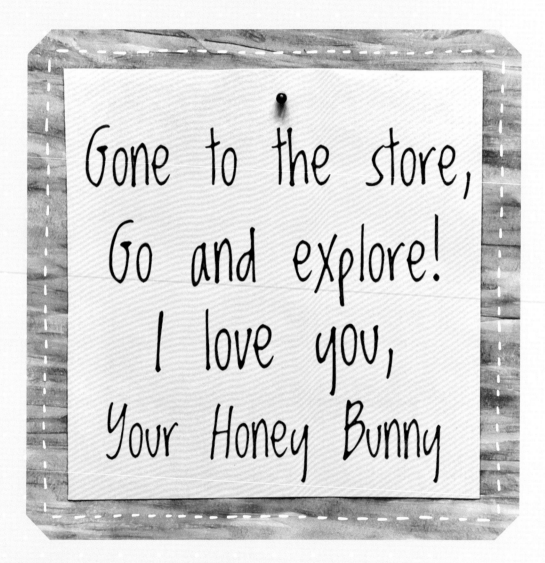

Gone to the store,
Go and explore!
I love you,
Your Honey Bunny

Patch smiled and thought, that's exactly what I will do!

Patch spied a giant rock near the house.
She ran over to it, climbed to the top,
and rested in the warm sun.

While Patch was relaxing on the rock,
a butterfly floated by. She watched
it skip from flower to flower.

Being curious, she climbed down
and followed the butterfly to
a field of bluebonnets.

Patch hopped into the middle of the beautiful, blue flowers
and discovered that they were as soft as a pillow.

Her tiny nose twitched as she sniffed the sweet flowers.

Patch continued to explore and stopped when
she came across a swing hanging from a tree.

She climbed in, but there was no one to push her.
So, Patch jumped down and headed back toward the house.

Patch noticed a red wagon and a basket of snacks.
Honey must have left these for me, she thought.

She looked around for someone to share the basket,
but no one was there.

Patch walked up to a cactus, decorated with sharp needles.
"Hello Mr. Cactus, do you like to explore?" she asked.

Mr. Cactus didn't respond.
He seemed to be pointing to a nearby tree.

Patch climbed the tree and found a bird nest
tucked into the arms of the tree's branches.

When she peeked inside, she saw two eggs.
"Hello," she said, but the eggs didn't respond.

Her ears perked up. In the distance, she heard a rooster crow.

"Cock-a-doodle do, where are you?" she called back,
and quickly climbed down from the tree.

Mr. Rooster was standing in the grass
at the base of the tree.
"How do you do?" he asked Patch.

Patch told him all about her day
in the Hill Country, but there
was just one thing missing.
"I'm looking for someone to share
my adventures."

"I'm on my way to visit some friends.
Would you like to go too?"
Mr. Rooster asked.

Patch nodded, hopped onto Mr. Rooster's back, and strutted down the path.

Soon they came up to a pig with wings standing next to a pink flamingo. Patch couldn't believe her eyes.

"These are my friends," Mr. Rooster said.

Mr. Pig and Miss Flamingo invited Patch
to join them in the big, green rocking chair
on the porch. She climbed into the chair
and sat between them.

Patch rocked and talked as she took in
the beautiful Hill Country view.

They were enjoying the sounds of the
birds chirping and squirrels chattering
when Patch heard her grandmother.

"Patch, Patch...time to come home,"
her grandmother said.

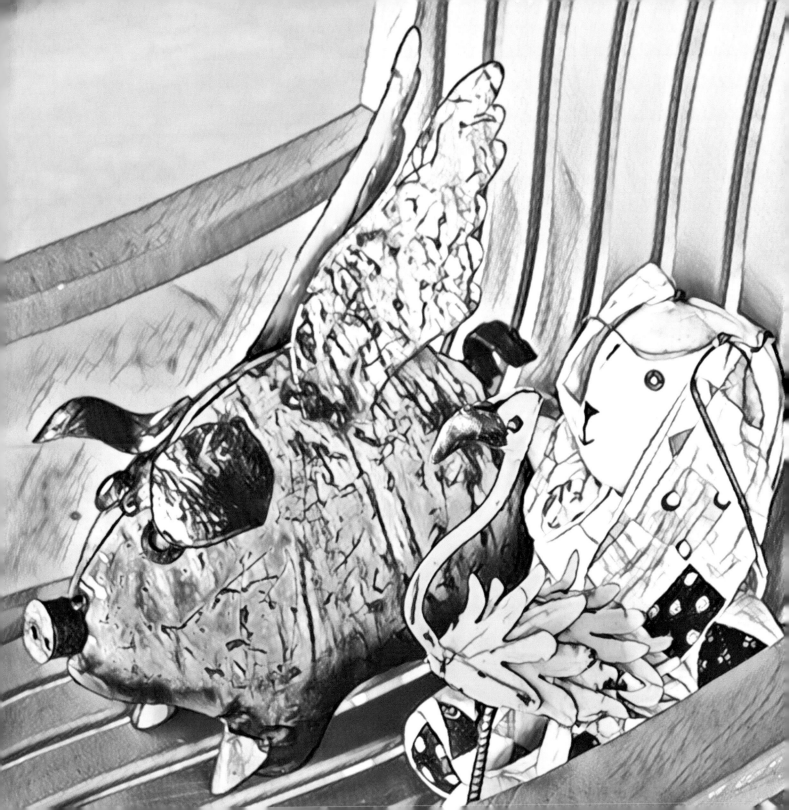

Patch bounced from the chair
and hopped back to Honey's house.

Her grandmother had a picnic set up
in the field of soft, green grass.

"Honey Bunny!" Patch exclaimed!

Patch told her grandmother about her exciting day.
Honey listened closely as Patch described the things she saw,
the sounds she heard, and the friends she made along the way.

Honey smiled and said, "You've become a true country bunny!"

When it was time to leave, Patch and Honey gave
each other a great big hug goodbye.

As Patch drove home,
she thought about her day.

She couldn't wait to visit her
grandmother again, because
that was where she first became
A Hill Country Bunny!